THE
WARBLERS

AMBER FALLON

Eraserhead Press
Portland, Oregon

ERASERHEAD PRESS
P.O. BOX 10065
PORTLAND, OR 97296

WWW.ERASERHEADPRESS.COM

ISBN: 978-1-62105-240-1

Copyright © 2017 by Amber Fallon

Cover art copyright © 2017 by Erik Wilson

Printed in the USA.

ONE

It was early on in the summer when Pa finally saw fit to do something about the warblers what had taken to living out in our back shed. He'd been putting it off all spring while we were getting the crops ready for planting, tilling the soil and the like. Not just by cause of the expense, you understand, although I'm sure that played a part in it. No, Pa's real hesitation came on account of the cure for warblers being damn near as bad as the disease, or at least that's what I'd heard tell of.

Before that summer, I'd never seen a Warbler for myself, less'n you count the dead ones they showcased during the county fairs over to Montgomery. Let me tell you, those dried up old shells were frightening enough without coming face to face with the live article when you went to the outhouse to do your business. Ma had that experience all to her lonesome but I reckon everyone in Hussock County heard her scream that morning. I never will forget the chill it sent down my spine to wake up in that fashion - hearing your own dear Ma scream fit to rattle a banshee. But even that wasn't enough to force Pa's hand. It wasn't until after my old sheepdog met her fate at the claws of the cursed beasts, leaving me to find what was left of my friend and companion that Pa finally agreed to take action. I do believe it was Ma's insistence at the end of things what caused him to respond and not so much the death of my dog, much as I'd like to think different. Womenfolk have a way of convincing the men in their lives to do whatever it is they want of them. It's the damnedest thing, really. I wonder what a wife'll get me to do one day what I don't have aim to.

The warblers had been a real nuisance before they had got to my dog, Ginger, but afterwards it was closer to home and heart. Ma was awful scared for my little sister Mabel, as she liked to go out back of the shed to pick wild flowers and chase butterflies all by her small self. I didn't like to ponder what could happen if she went out there and one of those things was waiting for her. My sister was young and sweet and didn't yet know the ways of the world. I don't believe there was a trace of fear in her pretty little head of those beasts or anything else. It was up to us, her kin, to protect and preserve her. It was a duty I took damned serious. As long as I was living, not a one of those things would come near to sight of her, let alone lay a claw on so much as a single blonde hair.

I know that Pa felt the same, and I'm sure that had some sway on his eventual decision, as well what Ma had been up to. All things spoke for, I did have cause to wonder just what it was my pa was fixing to do what had set his back up so hard in the corner. I knew that were it something effortless he'd have done it on the double back at the end of autumn when I first found trace of the beastly infestation. Not much more than scat and discarded bones back then, but I knew what it was clear sign of. Pa did, too. The day I'd taken him out to the back shed and shown him what I'd seen, I saw the careworn worry lines in his face deepen as he frowned. He'd tried hard to put it away in his mind like it was a light summer shirt, not needed until the air grew hot again, but try as best as he could, those things were still out there, still a menace to our farmland home and all who might come calling.

After months of fighting and cajoling the likes of which I'd never known my parents to do, it looked as though Pa would have to give in to Ma's insistence that he rid our farm of the warblers lest she pack up and take herself and Mabel to our relations out of fear of the dangers alone. Pa tried to convince her that they weren't that bad, really. Misunderstood, he called them, but from his own tone of voice it didn't ring true. He knew they were awful mean and nasty and he knew that sooner or later one of us'd find ourselves laid up injured or worse. Still he tried to fight it, but eventually he gave in. With a sigh and a scowl he turned his back on Ma and Mabel as they finished their breakfast of molasses and oats. He didn't glance in my direction as he passed by. He simply said, "Come on, boy, we're off to town."

TWO

Pa and I rode with Ben and Larry Scullory in the back of Ben's old clunker of a pickup into town to make the necessary arrangements. We didn't have a telephone at the house. In those days, few did. They were a modern convenience and quite the expense, or so I'd heard. Ma was none too keen on the idea, said it'd cause the neighbors reason not to come around to visit if they could just pick up a 'fool contraption' and send word that way. And so the call would have to be placed at McRory's General Store. It would cost two cents, something Pa was already complaining about as we bounced along the pitted dirt road. I listened to the pattering sound of gravel being thrown by the tires and felt the warm touch of sun on my skin.

Larry Scullory had a son, Nathan, who was near to my own age but we barely knew each other on account of him being military bound and me being nothing more than a simple farm boy. What I knew of Nathan could just about fill one of Ma's thimbles, but none of it was good. I'd heard he was mean as a junkyard dog and liked to pick a fight whenever the opportunity presented itself. Clyde Evans had lost his eye that way to Nate, or at least that's how the rumor went. I could recall seeing him a few times when we were younger, as the Scullorys did live on the next farm over from ours, but those memories were hazy with childhood. People liked to talk, and those tales may or may not have truth to them, I knew. But even as little as I knew of him, I had no love for Nathan Scullory. Ma had taught me from the time I was small not to be impolite or disrespectful at all, especially when a person wasn't present to defend themselves, so I always held my tongue when it came to news of Nathan Scullory and his accomplishments in the military. We saw his pa fairly often, my pa and I. At that time, community meant something and a man had to help his neighbors as they helped him, it was expected. Larry Scullory had been nothing but kind and helpful to us, and so I repaid that favor.

THREE

Larry mentioned our errand only once. Just before he started up the truck, the turn of the key making a noise like shaking a can full of rocks. He'd looked at my pa, real serious, and said in a low voice, "You know, Lang, you don't have to do it this way. My boy'll be back any day now. He's bound to have some rifles with him. I bet he could take care of your whole problem in a matter of hours. Be proud to do it, too, helping out his neighbors with his military ways and all."

My pa only shook his head in response.

Larry's face fell and he seemed to deflate like a balloon with a hole in it. After a minute he perked up and continued on as if nothing had happened.

Four

I could tell by the signpost on the corner that we were getting close to town. I was fit to bust with excitement at accompanying the menfolk on important business such as the matter of ridding our farm of the infestation of warblers. I had only been to town a few times in my life what I could recall and I felt the same sort of jittery excitement each and every time. I could not imagine what it must be like to live in a real city like Nathan did. I thought it must be the most glamorous and exciting thing in the world. I told Larry as much and he took his eyes off the road long enough to beam at me, swelling with pride at the mention of his son and the great honor that came with being a Military Family now. It pleased me to see that my talk could have such an effect on a grown man. I did not ever intend to mention my true feelings toward his son.

The day was bright and warm, and despite the business at hand, the terrifying monsters in our back shed couldn't have been further from my mind. I had in the pocket of my worn overalls my savings, which amounted to a wadded up dollar bill, a quarter, three pennies and a nickel all wrapped up in one of Ma's old hankies. It was practically a fortune to me then. I rubbed it between my fingers as if it were a mystical charm or ward against evil. I was wondering if I'd have time to spend my wealth before Pa swept us back to the farm and the plantings and waterings that had begun to fill my days, with only more to come as it marched on till summer. I had my heart set on a shiny new hunting knife and I aimed to spend a fair amount of time choosing one if I had my say, though the thought of going hunting without my dog by my side put an awful cramp in my heart. Life moves on, just as ever, even when we are forced to leave things we love behind. The knife wouldn't ease that, I knew, but it might take my mind off it for a while. Ma said that was just what I needed, and I do believe she was right. I couldn't think about anything but Ginger in the days since the accident. Sometimes I'd forget what had happened and I'd call to her out in the fields before I remembered she wasn't there to answer me. It weighed heavy on my heart when I remembered, and more than once I'd had to turn away to hide a tear or two that had begun to fall. Pa said I was being soft, and that there'd be a new dog for me once the money from the crops come in, but Ma knew how I felt. She helped me bury my dog under an old sycamore tree when Pa wasn't around. She and Mabel had even planted some flowers on the grave after I'd marked it with a piece of scrap wood I'd carved "GINGER" into with my pocket knife.

FIVE

Ginger'd been my companion ever since I could remember and it did things to me—unmentionable things that rotted out the pit of my stomach like an old melon—to see her that way, just a tangled pile of fur, bones, and bits of her insides, all that was left after those things had gotten through with her. I suppose it should've put the fear of them into me, but all it did was make me godawful angry. Angry at them, and angry at myself for letting my poor old dog out that night all those weeks ago. I well knew that those things liked to hunt after dark come on. After the sun would go down I'd hear them out there, back by the shed, shrieking their twisted warbling cries out there in the night, followed by the squeals of whatever prey they'd managed to hunt down, but Ma got mad something fierce if I kept Ginger inside of doors and she let her bladder go somewhere in the house. She was only supposed to go so far, just to relieve herself and come back inside, but you never can predict the whims of an animal. I didn't ever reckon she'd catch scent of something and run on out into the night. Once she'd left my sight I found I was too scared to go after her

15

and that just made me angrier at the whole mess. What good is a boy that can't even save his own dog? I felt a tear forming in the corner of my eye and that made the ball of anger in my chest burn like fire. I wanted those things dead and it couldn't happen fast enough. I only wished I could do it with my own two hands. I thought about it sometimes. Then I remembered what had happened to the Tate's boy, Lee, when he had tried to catch a warbler himself last summer when Mayor Connolly started offering a bounty on them. They hadn't found much more of him than shards of bone and bits of skin. His own mama didn't recognize him. I'd heard tell that they had to identify the body by the scraps of fabric from the clothing he wore. The mayor called off the bounty after that. Thinking about what had happened to that boy, not much younger than me, put visions into my head of my own Ma, tears in her eyes as she tried to remember what I'd worn that day, looking at scraps of bloody cloth held out to her by the constable. No, I didn't dare try anything that foolhardy by my lonesome. I wondered if maybe I should save my money and see if old Eddie Pickering would mount one up for me after they was killed like he did for Pa when he caught that big mouth bass last spring. I reckoned that would be a right fitting way to pay homage to my dog and to show for all who saw it that I wasn't afraid of no slimy, spineless old warbler.

We hit a bump and I looked up from my day dreaming, startled to see my pa staring at me like I'd been up to something shameful. I sighed and looked over the side of the truck at the gravel and dust as we drove over it, speeding past trees and signs like we were running from something.

SIX

A short time later, Larry slowed the truck so we could get ourselves out and walk the rest of the way into town. It wasn't a long walk, but it would take some time. I wondered if Pa would say anything about my day dreaming. It wouldn't be the first time he'd boxed my ears over what he called "Having my fool head in the clouds." I couldn't help my imagination. Sometimes I just thought up things and before I knew it, time had slipped away. I didn't mean for it to happen. It just did. Ma tried to defend me once or twice, but Pa would have none of it. That was where he chose to put his foot down. I didn't know what it was that burred him that way, but I felt ashamed of it nonetheless.

I stuck my hands in my pockets and waited for Pa. Larry told us he had some feed to pick up and would swing back by to get us once it was loaded. Pa and I nodded our thanks and took our leave. The walk was quiet. We didn't say nothing to each other. I reckon neither of us could think of anything to say. The air was growing hot and thick already. Bug chatter and bird calls came from the tall grass to either side of the dirt road. Pa and I saw a man just outside of town. I guess he was a preacher or something on account of the way he was dressed, all in black, balmy as it was, with a stripe of white at his throat. His white hair was wild and bushy and his eyes were all filmed up like something dead. I believe he had gone blind. It gave me a start when he grabbed my arm though. He seemed to see right into me with those white eyes of his and his grip was powerful cold despite the weather being so warm. He held my arm firm when I tried to pull away. Pa looked angry and I thought he might take a swing at him, but then the preacher man started to shake and his breathing quickened. He spoke through clenched teeth spraying spittle all foamed up like an animal what gone rabid. He said, "BOY! There are some things what are supposed to be left to the dark places!" Pa grabbed my other shoulder and pulled me loose. We left that man standing by the side of the road, trembling and spitting like he was possessed. Pa didn't know what to say I guess. I couldn't think of a thing either. I felt bad of it, but somehow I was relieved to have Pa's focus put on something other than the warblers or myself. Thinking of the warblers, my thoughts returned to what was waiting for me out in the back shed at home. Ma and Mabel were alone with those things for right now, and although I did know that they didn't like to hunt in the daylight on account of their sensitive little eyes, it made me worry. A knot formed in my stomach. In my head I saw the same scene as before, with the constable and the bloody scraps of clothing, only this time he was holding out bits of Ma's apron and Mabel's dress to Pa and me.

SEVEN

I didn't feel quite so excited anymore. Truth be told I was more eager now to get the whole matter over and done with than I was to buy me a hunting knife. I started to get this feeling like something Ma would have said was like someone standing on your grave. I didn't know much about what was done to get rid of warblers. Growing up as I did, they were always a threat, but before this summer I'd never had to worry much about them myself. They were always some other family's problem. I suppose that's the way it goes for everybody. Things like that are always someone else's problem; that is until they become your problem.

The whole thing was so exciting and new to me at the start that I hadn't given it much thought. Now I was thinking about it and I was getting mighty worried. The warblers were bad. Bad as any animal I had seen or heard tell of in my life. They were big and they were ugly and mean and they stunk something terrible. They made too much noise and tore things to shreds and killed and ate up livestock and even people when they could manage it. They had taken up residence in our shed sometime over the winter so there was no livestock to speak of for them to slaughter, thankfully, or else we'd have had that mess on our hands as well as poor old Ginger. We had sold our last cow to the Ellerys that fall and no more chickens until Pa could repair the henhouse. We had mouths to feed, Pa said, and that came before paying some fancy exterminator to clear out some pests. Ma and my baby sister were awful scared though. The two of them wouldn't go anywhere near that side of the house, daylight or no. I can't say as I blamed them, especially Mabel. She was only four years old and small enough that one big Warbler could carry her off and maybe swallow her up all by its lonesome. I hadn't seen a living one up close as yet, only the dead ones they displayed over in Montgomery come fair time. I knew the ones we had must be larger than those by the size of their scat and by the noise they made when they flew past my window at night, but just how much larger, I couldn't rightly say. If Pa had any indication, he wasn't telling. I knew he wanted me to be strong like he was and to "get my head out of the clouds". I wanted to make him proud of me, like all boys want of their fathers. I helped out when I could in the fields and with the farm like a good boy should, even when it pained me to do so. There were times when I wished I were smarter like the Ellery boy what went to get more schooling over to the fancy University in Redfield some years back, or strong and brave like Nathan Scullory, but I was plain old Dell McDale and that would just have to do.

By the time we reached McRory's the sun was up to

the top of the sky and sweat was pouring off Pa and I, soaking us through like we'd been dunked in the well. It felt good to get in out of the heat where the sun couldn't reach us. I could already feel my skin starting to turn a color, but I didn't mind. It would be good for me to get brown again instead of sickly and white like I had got over the winter. McRory's wasn't a big place, but it was stocked with damn well everything I could imagine. It was owned by a man named Ira McRory. He was tall, taller than my pa by a good bit, and broad in the shoulders, with light blue eyes and dark hair gone gray around the forehead. He ran a clean shop and did a good, honest business keeping the local farmers plied with everything from bolts of fabric for the women to make clothes from to seeds and saplings, guns and ammunition for hunting, and even kept a trade in sweets and paperback books. It was the latter I held more of a fascination with, ever since I learned how to read, though I knew better'n to let that on. Instead I stood by the counter and held my place as Pa marched in with his head held high. I watched him go, thinking how proud I was of the man what had raised me.

EIGHT

Pa bought us some sodas which was an unexpected treat. I drank mine down and felt the fizz tickle my tongue. It was cold and sweet. I wished I could share it with Ma and Mabel, fool thought that was. I knew it would be warm and flat by the time we made it home, but that didn't prevent me from feeling just a little twinge of guilt at the sweet I was enjoying without the company of my ma and sis.

I watched as Pa finished up his drink in one great swallow. He left me sitting on a stool in the front of the store by the soda fountains as he went to talk to Mr. McRory. I couldn't help but lean over and look in the direction of the hunting knives. They were lined up like soldiers in a glass display case hung on the wall. I finished my own soda, barely tasting the last few swallows and walked over to the case, leaving the empty glass on the counter with foam running down the insides. I had my eye on one of those fine pieces of steel in particular, a 7" long blade with a carved ivory hilt and little brass accents. It was a beauty of a knife, one I'd be mighty proud to call my own. I was imagining how it would feel in my hand, the heft of all that sharpened metal, when I overheard my father having an argument with Mr.McRory.

"You don't have to bring that kind of trouble down on us all, Langdon!" Mr. McRory was saying, "We don't need it, not on account of a few animals taken up living out back of your shed. Why for half a dollar, I bet you could hire those Haversham boys out Faterville way to do that job for you, keep it local."

Pa used his serious voice, "I don't aim to hire no Havershams, Ira. I don't like it none neither but it's got to be done. Now I paid you good money on the barrel head, you stand aside and let me make my call."

I could hear in Pa's voice that he wasn't going to be put off from what he'd come to do. That odd nervous feeling had come back to settle in the bottom of my stomach like a big old rock. I almost wished Mr. McRory would stop Pa from making his call and we could just go home to the farm and let everything lie as it was, but I knew that wasn't going to happen. Pa wouldn't back down, not when he'd given Ma his word. Mr. McRory sounded angry and afraid, and I knew that those were two powerful feelings, powerful enough to compel some men to do awful things to one another, but I knew that he was good and decent, and that he'd give in and let my Pa have his way.

Now I knew I shouldn't be eavesdropping like I was so you can believe I didn't want to be caught in the act. I near jumped out of my skin when Mr. McRory came from the back room where he kept the telephone. He didn't seem to notice me at all, though. He just looked at the floor like he was sad about something.

"Your father's a stubborn old fool," he said after a moment had passed.

That angered me.

"I won't hear you say not a word against my pa!" I said, turning towards Mr. McRory with a look that said I was fixing to fight.

But he just looked even sadder.

"I know, son, and I'm sorry." He put his hand on my shoulder and looked me in the eye. "Fear can do things to people. I can't claim to understand it myself, but I know what I've heard and it ain't good for none of us. You be careful, Dell, you hear? Your pa is sending your ma and sister over to Granby. See if you can't go with them. Don't be a fool, boy. Graveyard's full up with fools."

I didn't know what to say. I just stood there, looking at Mr. McRory and feeling fear and doubt growing in my heart. I didn't have to wait long, though. Pa came through the big double doors soon after. I couldn't read the expression on his face at all, and that scared me more than anything else so far had been able to. I always knew what my pa was thinking. Ma used to call us to peas from the same shell we were so much alike in some regards. To see him in a way that was unrecognizable put the fear in me beyond what I had thought possible. He walked past me, looking at Mr. McRory with something like disdain in his eyes, or maybe it was guilt. I couldn't be sure which one it was, but it damned sure wasn't brotherly love. "It's done."

was all that he said and I wasn't rightly sure to which of us he'd said it. He didn't slow down or wait for me, so by the time I realized he aimed to leave the store I had to run a bit to catch up with him.

"What happened, Pa?" I asked when I got close enough for him to hear me without having to shout. Looking at my pa, I suddenly realized just what it was he was feeling, and why I hadn't been able to recognize it before. My own pa was scared, and scared bad. He was putting on a brave face, I could tell that much, but he was more afraid than I had ever seen him. I felt cold all over at the realization.

"Some folks are gonna come over to the house." he said. Suddenly, he looked old in my eyes. Fear seized my heart like a cold vice and wouldn't let go. I took pause, afraid my feelings would leak through the surface like a missing roof tile would let rain leak in.

"What sort of folk?" I asked, not sure I wanted to know, "And when?"

Pa walked with his head down and moved more quickly than I believe was comfortable for him. My pa was in good shape, but farm work does take a toll on a man after he does it a good long while. My pa looked old and he looked weary. He didn't answer my questions, and I didn't figure it would be a bright idea to ask again so soon, so we went on in silence to wait for the Scullory brothers to pick us up and return us to home.

NINE

Despite how terrible hot it was outside, I had gooseflesh. Neither Pa nor I spoke a word to each other the whole way. It was a long, quiet walk and it gave me time to think about what had happened back in town. I looked for sign of the strange preacher man we'd seen before but it looked like he'd plum vanished. I didn't feel right about it. Looking around at the area where he'd been made his words come back to my head like lightning. "BOY!" he'd thundered, his fingers digging into my skin like the tines of a fork, "There are some things what are supposed to be left to the dark places!" What had he meant by that? Did he know about the warblers? I was sure if I said anything of it to Pa he'd tell me I was being a fool to listen to the ramblings of a sick old man. Instead I held my head low and trudged on down the path, wondering what the future held for me and my family.

TEN

Pa and I sat in the back of the pick-up truck with sacks of grain and corn and listened to the wind blow by us. I didn't want to be a bother so I held my tongue as best I could. I looked at my pa a few times but each time I did it just made me more scared of what I saw. I wished I knew more about who he had called and why everyone seemed to think it was such a terrible idea. The warblers were bad, I knew that much. I did know that if you just left them alone that they would breed and get out of control and infest other farms in the area, so it was hard for me to understand why everyone seemed so against getting rid of the damned things in whatever manner was necessary. I tried not to think about what kind of a thing could scare so many grown men but it was impossible to keep it off my mind for long. Dozens of visions flashed through my head; powerful men with fists the size of hay bales and muscles like oxen, wild Indian savages with exotic weapons carved from the bones of their enemies, gangs of game hunters with muskets and rifles that thundered like storm clouds rode across my imagination on steeds as black as night and as white as snow. I wondered who was coming.

Who could be so frightening they'd put so much fear into so many people? I reckoned whoever it was had to be strong and tough as rocks to handle getting rid of the warblers, but that didn't mean they were someone to be scared of. It had to be something else and I aimed to find out what it was. I thought about ways I could do that very thing as the truck drove on. Perhaps I had use for Nathan Scullory after all. His pa had said he'd be coming home soon. Maybe he knew more about the warblers and could tell me something helpful.

ELEVEN

"When will Nate be coming back home for a visit?" I asked Larry, breaking the long held silence.

My pa jumped when I spoke aloud but he tried to act like he hadn't. I pretended I didn't notice. Larry looked backwards into the truck bed where Pa and I were sitting on sacks of grain. I wished he wouldn't do that while he was manning the wheel of his truck. Didn't seem safe to me somehow, though I was sure if I'd said anything about it my pa would've died of shame right there. I had thought about what would happen if that truck hit a rock or somesuch and flipped over and spilled us all out on the road like my sister's scatter jacks, but those pictures were awful scary so I tried hard not to think on them too much.

Larry smiled back at me, the corners of his eyes wrinkled up and those wrinkles filled with the dirt and grime of a hard day's work so that they looked like dusty cobwebs on his red face when once again they settled. "Why, Nate's coming back for a visit just this very week. Should be here abouts tomorrow or Thursday I suppose. Are you wanting to see his new medals, son?"

I nodded, but I hadn't known anything from

Nathan's medals, new or old. No, I wanted to talk to him because I reckoned someone from the City would know better just who or what it was my pa done made a deal with. If he wouldn't tell me himself I would have to find out on my own.

Larry looked pleased and I reckon I couldn't hold it against him none for being a mite too proud of his own boy, despite my own feelings towards him. "I'll send him over once he gets here. After his Ma is finished with him, of course." Larry made a face what showed all too clear how he felt about the womenfolk and their ways.

"Thank you, Sir." I said, polite as could be.

Larry nodded and turned back to the road and I breathed a little easier, both on account of his driving and the idea that soon I might have answers. If whoever it was who was coming didn't do it before Nathan arrived.

My nerves were worn just about raw by the time we reached home. I could tell looking at Pa that he felt the same way. It was a strange feeling, seeing your pa like that. I had grown up feeling like my pa was the strongest, bravest man in the world, and here he was afraid of something I didn't understand. It made me feel old beyond my years. I wondered if this was what it felt like to be a grown man, seeing all that you knew put to ruin when you looked at it from the other side of childhood. I hoped not. If that was the case, adulthood looked to be mighty depressing in my eyes.

A short time later, Larry stopped the truck, prying

me from dreams about strongmen and ancient warriors. Pa and I climbed out over the gate this time so as not to upset all the grain what was stacked up so neat. We stood by the road a minute as the Scullorys drove away, Pa shading his eyes from the sun with one callused brown hand as he watched the truck clunk off down the road trailing a plume of dust. When it had rounded the corner that lead past our farm and onto Scullory ground, Pa turned back towards me. He put his strong hands on my shoulders and looked me right dead in the eyes. His face was somber, the fear I saw before gone now like a shadow at noontime. My pa was not a small man, and his likeness had been passed down to me. I was only fourteen but I was tall for my age, nearly as tall as my pa and taller than Ma by a hand's length. Pa's expression was grave, his eyes bore into me like worms in the loamy earth after a rainstorm. I felt a lump rise up in my throat.

"Dell," said Pa in a voice that I understood meant he was about to say something awful serious. I listened intently. "You're getting to be a man now, son, and a damned fine one at that." Despite how serious the tone had got, I couldn't help smiling. "I'm sending your ma and your sister over to your aunt and uncle's out there in Granby until the situation with the warblers is dealt with. I'd like for you to stay here and help me man the farm in their stead."

I thought about what Mr. McRory had said to me about that, but I knew I didn't much have a choice. Pa wanted me here on the farm and here was where I would stay whether I was afraid or not, which by that time I reckon I was. Part of me felt good about being handed such responsibility, and about being called a man by my father but another part of me was even more afraid, part of me felt like my father wanted me to stay so he didn't have to be alone to face whatever was coming to deal with the warblers and that seemed downright cowardly of him, me being just a boy and all.

What if Mr. McRory had been right and I'd be better off going with Ma and Mabel? What if something bad happened while they were gone? I'd never see them again, never see my sister grow up and marry off, let alone finding a wife for my ownself. It was awful hard to be thinking such things, worrying about what the future would bring and where it would leave us. I loved my pa something fierce, but the fear in my stomach over what might be coming made me feel sick and weak with worry.

I swallowed the lump in my throat. My pa needed me. I made up my mind right then and there that if something awful was going to take place that I wanted to be there, right beside my pa like a good son should be, to do what I could to protect us both and the home of our family.

TWELVE

I chose to swallow my fear and be the man my father wanted me to be, the one I hoped he saw in me. The one I hoped I'd become, though maybe not so soon as was being forced upon me. We don't chose our paths, Ma would say, the road we walk is chosen for us. I thought about asking Pa once more about what was going to happen and who he had called, but I thought better of it just then. Instead I nodded resolutely.

"Okay, Pa, whatever you think is best," I said.

He smiled then, but it was somehow sad.

"You're a good son," he said and squeezed my shoulder as we walked towards the house.

I was feeling dark and lonely though the sun was high still and beating down on us between the shadows of branches we passed under. I looked back over my shoulder one more time as we left, looking out to the road. I almost felt like something might be coming up behind me.

THIRTEEN

Supper the following night was the last meal we'd all be together for as a family until after the warblers had been dealt with. I didn't suppose I knew how long that would be, but the way Ma was acting it was fixing to be a while. I don't reckon she knew any more than I did, but she sure cooked up a storm. It seemed like everything to be had in the pantry had been boiled, baked, or stewed and laid out, either on the table or in boxes for Pa and I to eat after Ma and Mabel were with our relations. I suppose it was her way of dealing with the fear I knew she felt.

Pa looked at all of the food Ma had so lovingly prepared for us all and said, "This looks like a mighty fine meal. Fit for a king!"

Ma smiled back at him, though I could tell there was tension in the air all around. Everything felt forced, like it was some sort of a play put on for benefit of myself and Mabel. Mabel was sitting solemnly in her chair, looking at me with her big round eyes. I sure was going to miss her. Her and Ma both. Once again I hoped the whole mess would be over soon.

We ate our meal mostly in silence, no one wanting

to say what was really on our minds. There were a lot of painted on smiles around that table. I supposed that if something horrible were to occur, it would be better for those of us what lived through it to remember them that didn't with smiles on their faces.

I wasn't accustomed to thinking such dark thoughts. It chilled me that in such a short time I had taken to it as naturally as a fish to water.

After a time, I supposed everyone had finished eating. We sat in silence with our stomachs full but our hearts strangely empty for a stretch before Ma got up and began to clear the table. It was almost like breaking a spell. Pa stood up, wiping crumbs from his mouth with an old hanky before tucking it back into his pocket. Mabel began to fidget in her chair, shifting and reaching for things on the table. I moved to help Ma clean up, but she shooed me away, so I went outside to watch the sunset before dusk came on and the warblers woke up, mean and nasty as ever, all leathery wings and claws and hunger.

I stood on our rickety old porch, looking out towards the peeling paint on the back shed as the sunset drained like a stuck pig, bleeding out red all over. A gentle little breeze blew up, whispering in the grass and lifting my hair a bit as it came. The earth smelled clean and right, but underneath it I could catch scent of the warblers, a sick sweet smell like rotting meat mixed with the stink of the outhouse in the heat of summer. I listened hard, straining to hear the monsters moving inside the shed from where I stood, but all I could hear was the wind and the sounds of Ma tending to the washing up inside.

How many warblers were out there? I wondered. How many had it taken to kill and eat up my dog? How many would it take to do the same to me? My fists clenched around the old wooden railing, splinters coming off in my hands as flakes of old paint fell to the dirt below. I wanted them dead. I felt bad for that, in all honesty, but I couldn't change the way I felt. Ma and Father Timmons said we should wish ill on no living creature, but those things had killed my dog and I knew in my heart they'd kill my sister, my ma, and everything I had ever loved if they only got the chance. How could I keep from hating them? How could I hear them every night and not dream of seeing our land strewn with their dead bodies, our shed finally clear, and our home once again safe for Mabel to play at her whim?

I had turned to go back inside when I spied Nathan Scullory over to the side of the house. He was taller than he had been when I last recalled seeing him, and he'd grown more muscular. His face was scrunched up all mean and angry. He wore a grey military hat with pants to match and shiny black boots, but his shirt was a torn up old white undershirt what looked like the ones my pa wore beneath his church clothes. It looked like he was fixing to throw a rock clean through my window. When he saw me he dropped it, but the mean old dog expression never left his face. He turned towards me, puffing his chest up and clenching his fists, walking his meanest walk on his way to the porch.

He was exactly as I had remembered him in form if not in frame. I went over to the porch rail, steeling myself against whatever insults old Nathan might throw in my direction. I tried to stay calm and let my curiosity over his visit and my fear of what he might get up to if I let myself be provoked hide in the corners of my mind.

"Hello, Nathan," I said, trying to be cordial. I wasn't sure what it was he wanted but I knew he could whip me in a fight one handed and I didn't aim to start no trouble, not with the mess what had already been given me.

Nathan and I had never been the best of friends, though I bore him no ill will and no cross words was ever spoke between us, at least none that I could recall. Nathan wasn't as tall as I was, though he was two years older, but he did have a lot more muscle than I did on my wiry frame. He had dark hair and eyes and a flattish face what looked like someone had smacked him square in it with a shovel. With my own sandy blond hair and blue eyes, we were about as different as could be lookswise.

"Evening, Dell," He said, and I got the idea that he was sizing me up. "My pa said you wanted to see me about my medals. I figured that was a lie but I decided to come see what you wanted for myself. I reckoned you'd be inside of doors by now, what with them warblers you got back there." He gestured with his chin towards the rear yard, which had grown shadowy in the evening light. "I was just going to throw a rock to get your attention."

I nodded, sticking my hands deep into the pockets

of my overalls. "Yeah, we got warblers alright," I said. "They killed my dog. Ate her up but proper. Left a real mess, too."

How I ever managed to speak those words without a tremor in my voice I'll never know, but I was grateful to whatever got me through it. Nate nodded in sympathy. I imagine he knew how much I had loved that dog. There's a sort of universal law of boys and their dogs and I felt that Nate understood just what it was I had lost. It became easier to speak to him after that.

"It's the warblers I wanted to speak to you for," I said, climbing over the porch rail and jumping to the ground to stand face to face with Nathan Scullory. He was much bigger up close than he had been even from just a few feet away and I could smell sweat and the dirt and dust of the road on him. His eyes were like little chips of flint, small and cold and hard.

"What about them?" Nathan asked, tilting his head in query, causing his hat to shift a little to one side.

"Pa's called someone to come get rid of them. I don't rightly know who or what, but I know from everyone's reactions around town that it can't be good. I want to know what I'm in for," I said, casting a glance once again over my shoulder.

Nate rubbed his jaw thoughtfully. "I can't say as I know much about warblers myself. Those are a country problem, to be sure. In the city the worst we get are the trash can rats. But I do think I know what your pa has gone and done."

I could only stare in response as I waited for Nathan to continue.

He paused for a minute, looking over to the shed before he went on, gesturing like our schoolmarm, Miss May, back when I did my learning at the little one room schoolhouse. There were fond memories of simpler times, bringing my knapsack with dusty chalk and a chipped slate, Ma packing my lunch, catching snakes and toads what to frighten the girls with. I wished I could go back there a spell, if only just to distance myself from the matters at hand.

"Warblers are a lot like birds," he said. "Big, ugly, meat eating birds, but birds just the same. The natural predators of birds is reptiles, one reptile in particular in regards to those beasts. It's called a Squamate. I've never seen one myself, so I don't know rightly what to expect, but I do reckon that's what your pa done called to have brought here, and why all the folk around are afraid. The Squamate's supposed to be big and fierce and meaner than a mamma badger. I've heard tell one could take a man's head off with the flick of a tail or the swat of a claw."

I couldn't decide at first if Nathan was just trying to put the fear into me, or if he was serious. I searched his face for some sign of the truth. He looked genuine, his dark eyes were solemn and his expression seemed sincere. I tried to get my mind around the idea, but found that I couldn't. My pa had called someone to deliver to us some sort of beastly reptile what would eat up the warblers? What then, after it had ate its fill?

Would it eat other things? Say, human beings? How could we control it? Would it come with handlers? I had more questions, but I didn't think Nate had any answers for me and I sure didn't want to push his good will no more.

"If that's what's coming, I want to be here to see it," Nathan said, an edge creeping into his voice.

He was a military cadet, so I understood his bravery and his interest, especially if that beast was all he had said it was.

I nodded, thinking that if the Squamate truly was a thing to be afraid of it wouldn't be bad having another hand around. Nathan had a gun and judging by his medals, he knew how to use it.

"I don't know what's going to happen, or when, but I reckon you'd be as welcome as any to come see it."

Nathan shook his head. "Not if my pa hears that's what I'm aiming to do, I won't."

Nathan looked me right in the eye and raised his finger to my chest, a scowl once again screwing up his face just as mean as a nasty old witch.

I sensed there was a sort of threat behind his gesture so I stayed still, planted where I was. "You find out when that thing's coming and you let me know just as soon as you can. I'll tell my pa I'm going to see some friends out to Brewster but I'll be by here to see what's what."

Nathan withdrew his prodding finger from my chest but his face remained in a snarl. His posture was like a dog just looking for a fight but I didn't intend on giving him any reason to start one. If that was what he wanted, that was what I'd do.

Now I don't condone lying, but I also don't go around telling other folk in what manner to act, so I just nodded. I'd find out if I could and pass the information on. Truth was, now that I had an idea of what was coming to my small farm, I felt a lot safer having a Military Man around, even if it was just old Nate Scullory.

Nathan's eyes kept darting back to the shed, and I got the feeling he was getting awful nervous as the night come on. He turned his gaze back to me and said, "Well, I guess I'll be seeing you."

He tugged on the brim of his hat in a gesture of farewell, turning as he did and putting me between himself and the rear yard.

I wondered if that were a purposeful act or just the way he'd intended on moving. I nodded, though he couldn't see it, and stood there in the side yard willing myself to be steady until he was out of view.

Full night had come on in those last few minutes I'd been speaking with Nate and off in the distance, but still too close for comfort, the warblers had begun their cries, warning all those around, folk and animal alike, that they were looking for a meal.

I ran for the door, slammed it behind me, and threw the latch just as quick as I was able. Ma looked startled when I come in in such a fashion, her green eyes going round as saucers. I guess I'd never realized how pretty Ma was. It made me a little sad that before now I couldn't really remember when last I'd stopped to look at her. Folks said I took after Pa and Mabel took after Ma, which I guess was a good thing. My sister would grow up like her, willowy and graceful with a wide smile full of kindness and light. Ma dried off her hands on her apron before untying the strings and hanging it over the little cast iron stove to dry. She hugged me close, tears were in both our eyes, though I tried to hide it. She had never felt so fragile or so precious as she did right then. I didn't want her to leave. It was on my lips to beg her not to when she let go of me and stepped back. She looked up at me, trying to force a smile. For whose benefit, hers or mine, I couldn't be sure.

"It'll be alright in a little while, Dell," she said, her voice soft. "You'll see. Your sister and I won't be gone much more than a heartbeat."

I smiled back, nodding and wondering if that was the last time I'd see my mother. I couldn't seem to help what grim thoughts had come over me, though I didn't like them one bit.

"Won't you come on and help us with our things?" she asked.

I nodded and followed her to the front room where Mabel was already waiting, clutching her dolly in one hand and a little hanky tied up with all her treasures in the other.

"Ma," she said when we come in, "Can Dell come with us?"

I leaned down and picked her up, scooping her into my arms. "I'm gonna stay and help Pa out with the farm," I said. "Can you take care of Ma in my stead?"

Mabel nodded solemnly, her eyes round and serious. "I'll watch over her."

I hugged my sister close, taking in the scent of her, like rose water and the powdered soap Ma used, before setting her on the ground. I wanted to remember her just that way.

Ma and I took hold of the suitcases she had stacked so carefully and carried them out to my Uncle Errol's wagon waiting on the front path. Mabel toddled along behind us as we went.

When we got out to the wagon, Uncle Errol was standing up against it, chewing on a wad of tobacco. He smiled and straightened when he saw me.

"Why, Dell!" he said, somehow managing to sound cheerful despite the circumstances, "if you aren't the spitting image of your father when he was your age!"

He took one of the suitcases from me and clapped me on the back, putting an arm around my shoulder and leading me onward. We loaded everything up and tied it down proper as Ma and Mabel got settled into the carriage. Errol pulled me aside just out of hearing range of the womenfolk.

"You know," he said, leaning down to whisper, "I tried to talk your pa out of this foolishness."

Errol was a good bit taller than my pa, though the two were brothers, and he didn't look much like him save for the crook of the nose they both shared. He was as tall and gangly as my pa was wiry and strong, much like me.

"I know," I said, looking back to the house.

Pa was inside, but I didn't think he was apt to come out. I figured it best to let him alone. I supposed he and Ma had already said their goodbyes, at least I hoped they had.

"I don't know why for he feels compelled to do this." Errol scratched his head. "At least he had the good sense to get your Ma and your sister out of harm's way."

I nodded again, not sure what to say. I wouldn't speak ill of my father, not even to one of our relations, but I owed my uncle the respect of listening to his words whether or not I agreed with them. I reckoned I didn't know enough to judge either way.

"Why don't you come with us, Dell? Leave your old man to his fool errand. Plenty of room and I bet your cousins would be tickled to death to see you."

"I don't suppose I can do that, sir," I said, standing straighter. "My place is here, on this farm, with my pa."

Errol nodded like that was what he'd expected me to say.

"You're a good boy, Dell," he said, reaching out for my hand. "Don't you let anyone tell you none different."

He shook my hand firm before climbing up to his spot on the wagon. The horses pawed the ground fearfully, whinnying and shaking their heads. I could see little bits of white around the edges of their eyes. I supposed they could scent the warblers as most animals can smell predators nearby. They looked awful spooked at any rate, and I only hoped they wouldn't startle none on the ride back to Granby. I knew I was borrowing trouble, as Ma would say, but the dark thoughts were there again and I didn't know how to shake them free.

With a final nod of his head, my uncle cracked the reins. The carriage pulled away and I stood there looking after it, not even fear of the warblers could tear me away from the sight. I watched it roll off into the distance until I could see it no more before I turned to go back into the house, tears falling from my eyes. I wondered if there was a limit to the tears a man could shed in his lifetime and what happened once he'd used up his allotment.

FOURTEEN

Pa was sitting at the table when I came in, which startled me. It didn't look to me like he had noticed my entrance. He had a bottle open and a glass was sitting next to it. Judging by his expression, he'd filled and emptied that glass a few times already. Pa wouldn't have been drinking out in the open like he was if Ma and Mabel were still here, I reckoned. I don't suppose it mattered much. He looked up from his glass when I sat down next to him.

"Pa?" I asked, trying not to choke on the vapors wafting off the brown liquor in the glass he was holding.

Pa shifted in his seat, draining the glass dry and setting it back on the table with a clunk.

I tried a different approach to get my questions answered, hoping that perhaps the liquor would be of help to me. "Now that the womenfolk have left and it's just you and me, can we talk about that phone call you made over at McRory's?"

Pa swallowed hard and looked at the bottom of his glass like he hoped to see answers there or a maybe way out. Finally, after a long while, he sighed. "I reckon we can," he said sadly.

I sat patiently, waiting to see if Pa would pour another glass, or maybe even offer me some of the brown liquid, but he didn't.

"There are times," he said, "when there ain't no choice left to a man but to do a thing he doesn't want to do."

I nodded, but I didn't really understand what he meant. I thought on his words while I waited for him to continue.

"Pa?" I asked again after a time, deciding to take the direct approach instead. "What's coming to our farm?"

Pa swallowed again, and I wondered if the liquor had hurt his throat somehow. I couldn't imagine why a man would want to drink a thing what made the eyes water in such a way, but I had to admit that I wanted to try it to find out.

Pa leaned forward, resting his hands on his knees. He stayed that way so long I thought he might have nodded off, but finally he spoke, his voice soft and somehow frail. "It's called a Squamate, son."

I nodded. Nathan had been right.

"I saw one once, when I was a boy not much younger than you are now. Infestation of warblers down at the grain silo my Pa shared with some other farmers. I don't reckon I'll ever forget that day. Terrible beast."

Pa shuddered, his shoulders hitching like a sob. His speech was slurred, and his head was rolling to one side like he was nodding off. I thought he might be. Still, I hoped he would continue his story, but he remained quiet, almost dozing where he sat.

"When is it coming, Pa? Can you tell me that?" I asked once I was sure he was done with speaking of his past.

Pa stood up, took a second to gain his footing, and wiped his mouth with the back of his hand.

"Tomorrow. Round about dusk. Now get to bed, Dell. We've got a full day ahead of us. I reckon we'll both be needing our sleep."

I nodded, though Pa didn't see. He had already turned to go upstairs to the little room with the flowery yellow wallpaper he and Ma usually shared. He'd be alone in it tonight, though, and I reckon missing Ma a lot more than I was.

I went to my room after putting away Pa's glass and bottle. Though I was tempted, I did not try his liquor for myself that night. Afterwards I sat at the table in the chair where Pa had sat. I took comfort in the warmth of it as I thought about what was yet to come. Pa seemed afraid of the Squamate just as much as anyone. So why had he summoned it? I remembered what Mr. McRory had said about the Havershams. Why hadn't Pa at least talked to them first? Then I thought again of Lee Tate. I supposed being the man he was that my pa didn't want any casualties under his name. That big old Squamate could take care of itself, I reckoned, and even if not, I didn't believe anyone in town would miss it none. After a time my imagination had run out on me and my eyelids began to feel heavy. I didn't know how I'd ever be able to sleep, but I went up to my room anyway. I stood at the window for a spell, staring out into the darkness, straining my eyes to catch sight of the warblers, the wretched beasts what had brought all this about, tearing up my family and slaughtering my dog.

I changed out of my day clothes and lay down underneath the covers, my back to the window. Let them come, I thought, let them come and see what we have waiting for them. The last thought I had before I drifted off to sleep was of Ma and Mabel, returning to home and Pa and me there to greet them among a whole field of dead warblers laid out to dry like bales of hay.

I didn't get much sleep that night. Between tossing and turning and listening to the warblers outside, I couldn't manage to keep my eyes closed for too long. I got up out of bed and stood at the window, staring out at the rear yard in the direction of the back shed, lit up as it was by silvery moonlight. Every now and again I'd catch a glimpse of something dark and shadowy out the corner of my eye, but every time I'd look in that direction the shadow had disappeared like a ghost or a nightmare. Those things out there were all too real, but they'd be gone soon enough, I hoped. I just wasn't sure what else might be lost in the process.

FIFTEEN

The hours passed, as hours often do, and I was up and ready before the sun come up. I had a meager breakfast of biscuits, jam, and hardboiled eggs prepared for us by the time Pa had awoke. He came downstairs, looking like he'd had just about as much sleep as I had got, only he was worse for the wear. There were dark, puffy bags under his eyes and what looked like three days' worth of beard stubble on his lined face. Even his hair looked greyer. He sat down and we ate our meal in silence, neither one of us daring to speak a word of what we knew was yet to come. We had chores to do, and the rest of the day to face yet, though I didn't know quite how I'd manage. My stomach was all tied up in knots, so much so that I had begun to regret eating breakfast.

After Pa finished eating, I cleared the table. Somehow along the way I dropped and broke a water glass, and when I bent down to retrieve the shards I cut myself. Bright red blood sprang to the surface of my finger. I stood and looked at it, watching as it grew into bigger and bigger drops before rolling down my hand and dripping onto my shoe. Once again it felt like an omen. I wasn't the superstitious sort, not like

Ma was, but I suppose some of her sayings might have rubbed off sometimes and stuck with me. I couldn't shake that feeling, like someone had walked across my grave. I shook myself and chalked my jitters up to the excitement of the upcoming day. I finished with the dishes and cleaning up the broken glass before I went outside to help Pa fix up the side yard.

Sixteen

Pa and I spent the morning repairing the henhouse. It was hot, dirty work made worse by the fact that we were very near to the back shed. All the while we toiled I could hear those things in there, shifting and moving around and occasionally warbling softly in their sleep. Once in a while one of them would start the others off and there'd be a fight amongst them, screeching and scrabbling and making all kinds of commotion. I could smell them, too. A terrible odor like the henhouse when it needed to be cleaned, mixed with the stench of dead animals left out in the sun and Pa's brown liquor. Pa pretended he didn't notice it and I did the same, although the only ones we were fooling were ourselves.

Our next task would be to clean out the barn, but before we started on that, I asked Pa if I could go see Nathan Scullory. If Pa thought there was anything odd about my request, he didn't let on. Instead, he suggested I take one of Ma's pies as a gift to Mrs. Scullory. It would go bad if not, he reasoned, by cause of the fact that neither of us had much of a sweet tooth, even if we had felt like eating.

I went inside to wrap up the pie and I watched Pa

through the window. He stood near the henhouse we had just fixed up and stared towards the back shed for a while, then he sat down on a stump and wiped the sweat from his brow with an old bandana he carried with him just for that purpose. I brought him out a glass of water before I left on my way to the Scullory's. I stood there beside him while he gulped it down in two long swallows.

"Thank you, son," he said, handing me back the empty glass.

"You're welcome, Pa," I said, looking once more towards the back shed.

Whatever was going to happen, it was going to happen whether I liked it or not. I just hoped it happened soon. I was missing Ma and Mabel something fierce, and that feeling I had been getting, like something cold and dark come over me, was getting worse by the minute.

I rinsed the glass and set it on the wire rack next to the sink before picking up the pie and heading out to the road and the Scullory place beyond. I wasn't sure what I was going to say when I got there, but I would figure it out on the journey. All I needed to do was to find a way of informing Nathan that the Squamate would be coming that evening without his folks catching wise. I still didn't like the idea of his lying to them, but I wanted him there sure as anything. Truth be told I think I just didn't want to face whatever was going to happen all by my lonesome. I knew Pa would be there, but that was different. The past few days when

I looked at my pa, I saw how old he was, how worn around the edges and just plain beat up. It offered me no comfort to have him at my side when I was afraid. Matter of fact, I felt almost like I'd have to take care of him. Nathan was closer to my age and he was in the military. He was the best protection I reckoned I was liable to get.

As I walked down the road to the Scullory's, my thoughts weighed heavy on me. What was the Squamate, and why was everyone so powerful afraid of it? What would it do to the warblers? Eat them, I supposed. But all of them? Just how big was it? I pictured some kind of a dragon like the ones on the covers of books I had seen at McRory's. Would there be more than one Squamate? What would happen after it ate up its fill? I didn't know the answers to any of those questions, only thing I did know was that time would be the only way to find out.

SEVENTEEN

I was just about halfway to the Scullory place when my thoughts turned to calling Nate's motives into question. I had been thinking only of myself, which is an easy habit for one to get into. As it was, I just saw to the end of my own nose, as Ma would've said. Nate Scullory had to have a reason to be so keen on catching sight of the Squamate, and I was starting to wonder just what that was. I wasn't a devious sort, myself, so I had a hard time with managing to think like them that were, but the thought occurred to me that perhaps Nathan wanted to kill the Squamate, to prove his mettle to the menfolk and show the whole of our little community how brave he was. That was a terrible thought, but it had a ring of truth to it nonetheless. The notion brought a sickness into my stomach and right then and there I decided I would have no part of it, not even if it meant facing that creature all by my lonesome. I supposed there must've been some of my pa in me after all.

I stopped dead in my tracks and turned around to head back to home when Nathan Scullory came out of the bushes in front of me. His eyes were narrowed to mean little slits and he had his rifle slung over one shoulder. For the first time, I found myself afraid of old Nate in earnest.

"Hello, Dell," he said, taking the pie from my hands and unwrapping it before digging into it with his fingers.

It was red gooseberry, I saw. Ma's favorite. The filling looked gory and gruesome as Nate shoveled it into his mouth, pausing to lick his fingers in a way that made me think of a wolf eating from a fresh calf carcass.

"Just where are you going on this fine afternoon?"

I sensed there was real menace behind his words. Menace and maybe intent. I couldn't keep my eyes from straying to the barrel of his rifle. I wondered if he'd ever shot a man but I was far too afraid to ask him outright, not that I believed he'd tell me the truth, anyway.

"You wouldn't have been coming to talk to me about the Squamate, would you?" he asked as he dug once more into Ma's pie with his filthy fingers.

I stood silent, watching Nathan eat the pie my ma had prepared with her own dear hands. Somehow the way he swallowed, barely stopping to taste her hard work seemed disrespectful to her.

"Not chickening out, are you Dell?" he asked around a mouthful, poking me in the chest with a gooseberry covered finger.

It left a red mark on my overalls, right about where my heart would be, if I recalled correctly. I didn't like that imagery, not one bit.

"No, I went up to your place. I left when I didn't find you at home," I lied, and I was mightily uncomfortable with even the notion of it, but I had no other thought come to mind and I was in a terrible state of panic right about then.

Nate seemed to accept that. He nodded and ate some more of the pie. The hole he'd dug in the middle had begun to look an awful lot like my poor old Ginger. I thought I might be sick at the sight of it if I looked too long, brought that image back to mind, so I tried to keep my eyes aimed at another location. The only other place I could think to look was Nathan's gun, which started my mind running off in other directions.

"You find out when that creature's supposed to get to your place yet?" Nathan asked, looking me square in the eyes.

Even though I was a good bit taller than he was I felt like he was somehow looking down to me.

"Yessir," I said, showing him more respect than I ought've. "Round about dusk."

I stared down at my shoes. I hadn't wanted to give Nate that information, but I couldn't see a way out of doing so, and I couldn't have lied to him then even if I'd wanted to.

He looked at me for another long minute during which time I felt like my heart had stopped beating, before he finally nodded his head. "I'll be seeing you then," he said, "Dusk."

That last word sounded almost like a threat. With a curl of his lip and a nod of his head, Nathan walked past me towards his homestead, pushing the mostly eaten pie into my chest as he went. The red filling spilled down the front of my overalls like it was my insides and I'd just been shot. That thought was more than a mite too gruesome for me. I just hoped it didn't foretell of something yet to come.

When I got back home I found I was too ashamed to tell Pa what had actually transpired on the roadway. I was ashamed of my actions, ashamed of telling Nathan what I had, and worried about what my pa would do with that information, so I lied once more and told him I'd fallen in the road, and that I'd not found the Scullorys at home. There was an awful pit growing at the bottom of my stomach, but just which of the things what was weighing on me was the greater cause of it I couldn't be sure.

EIGHTEEN

On a farm, there's about always work to be done, and ours was no exception. The day went by quicker than Pa or I had noticed, and after what felt like no time at all, the sun started to lower itself in the sky. I looked over at Pa and he looked back at me and without a word we made our way to the front steps to wait for our visitor in grim silence. As we stood, staring towards the road, a shadow crossed over the sun, casting our small piece of the world into momentary darkness. I was shook up so bad that I took a step much closer to Pa, who pushed me back. I supposed once again that he wanted me to be brave, so I stood off to the left of him, trying to get my bearings. We stood for what felt like hours, watching as the shadows stretched and darkened. I hadn't seen hide nor hair of old Nate Scullory, and for that I was glad.

I was just about to open my mouth to ask Pa what time he thought our visitors might show up when I spied something off in the distance. All I could do was point Pa's vision in that direction.

From where we stood, it looked somewhat like a big old fancy stage coach like the ones what sometimes brought the moving picture shows to Montgomery Center, only it was painted all dark, so dark that it didn't seem to catch a glint of light off of the fading sun, but to swallow it whole. Dark as the bottom of a well, I thought. As it drew nearer, I noticed that there weren't no horses, and the coach seemed to float all by itself somewhat up above the road. The wheels didn't touch the ground somehow. They didn't even finish, they just sort of faded into wisps of sooty smoke before they ever reached the earth.

That coach moved awful fast, faster than anything I'd ever seen before. I was only vaguely aware that Pa had put his arm around my shoulder and was digging into my flesh with his fingers, his grip so tight his knuckles were near about white and my shoulder felt like it had been caught up in a vice. The coach drew up to a stop in front of us, but nothing broke the spell of silence what come upon us both since it had come into view. Somehow without even a door to open up, three figures appeared before us. Two were great big giants of men, or what looked like men, anyways. At least somewhat like men. Their skin was all gray like the marble on an old tombstone and it cracked in places around their mouths and eyes, showing through a bit of what was underneath, what looked like fire and brimstone. Their hair was a paler shade of gray and it faded away at the ends like smoke or fog the way the wheels on their carriage seemed to do. They weren't twins, I supposed, but definitely relations, quite probably brothers from the looks of them. Broad foreheads and sharp noses in between wide cheekbones and strangely delicate ears what came to points at the top. They were dressed like the cowboys I had seen on the covers of the pulp westerns at McRory's, only the colors were all wrong. Their hats were the color of charcoal, and below the shadow of the wide brims, their eyes glowed red like embers. They wore long coats the color of dried mud, and the only bright thing about their outfits was their matching red bandanas, which were a shade too bright to be natural or of this earth. Unlike their conveyance, their feet touched the ground good and proper, ending in pairs of matching cowboy boots what looked far too shiny, with huge, mean looking black spurs clinging to the backs. They were smiling, but there was no mirth there, only mire. Their teeth were too white, too straight, and far too sharp and their smiles were too wide to belong to real men of the earthly kind. Held between the two of them was the most magnificent beast I had ever seen with my own eyes.

The Squamate was not what I had been expecting. It was something I couldn't have imagined in my wildest dreams or my most terrifying nightmares. It stood upright, like a man, though it was a good deal taller than Pa or I or even Uncle Errol. It came about to the shoulders of the men who carried it, its handlers, I supposed. It wore clothes like a man, at least in part. A long, thin tail what reminded me of a snake peeked from beneath a long coat like the ones worn by what I had taken to calling the Charcoal Cowboys in my mind, for no other name seemed fitting. The Squamate's coat was of a soft yellow color like pollen and hung loose on its slender frame. Above its eyes, huge round pools of swirling gold and green near to the size of dinner plates, sat a brown broad brim hat. A gray bandana wrapped around its mouth and nose like one of those bandits I'd seen at the motion picture show, which was at odds with the bright green scales what covered its body. They looked hard as stone and shiny and smooth as glass. It had enormous thighs with muscles that rippled like water in a stream when it moved. The air all around it felt like being outside during a thunderstorm, charged with energy that made my skin tingle and my hair stand on end. Just being near to it gave me gooseflesh. Up in front of it, the creature held its hands—or maybe they were claws—out stiff. I could not see what they looked like, for they were encased inside a large metal box with a gigantic keyhole out in front. Rivets the size of half dollars stood out on the edges of that box, and I supposed it must be awful strong. For that I was doubly as glad.

NINETEEN

I had not realized that I had been holding my breath until I had begun to feel lightheaded. I gasped, sucking in air, and Pa startled, turning his head around quick to face me. I could see the fear in his eyes. I knew mine must've looked about the same. We were both fighting our instincts, the urge to run and flee. I thought of the horses in front of my uncle's carriage and how they had looked on smelling the warblers. I imagine we must've looked about the same way.

TWENTY

One of the charcoal cowboys held out his huge hand to Pa, cracked palm facing up, and said, "Payment for services due," in a voice what sounded like rock scraping rock and somehow vibrated the very air itself. I could feel those words echo right through my chest as if it was hollow and it made my bowels feel loose. I thought for a moment I might faint, but I held myself steady.

Pa stepped forward and placed a small leather pouch into the man's outstretched hand. It jingled lightly as it settled. The cowboy's grin widened until it took up most of the lower part of his face, an effect which terrified me right to my very core.

My heart was beating so fast I don't know how it kept up with itself. The Charcoal Cowboy closed his fist around the money and when he opened it again, all that remained was a small puff of smoke.

His brother removed from the folds of his coat a big old iron key with which he unlocked the metal box the Squamate held up in front of it. Both brothers had to hold it steady while the big reptile pulled its claws out, which was my first indication of just how god awful strong the Squamate really was. Its claws, I saw, looked much like hands, save for the fingers being far too long and tipped with what looked almost like shiny metal arrowheads. I had no doubt of what Nathan had said about it being able to take off a man's head with a swipe of one.

The Squamate issued forth a low, menacing hiss as it walked slowly towards the rear yard, as graceful as a dancer. It drifted past Pa and I, lifting its nose in the air like a coonhound smelling out the bog.

I saw something out the corner of my eye and, rattled as I was, I near jumped out of my skin. I turned my head to look and saw Nathan Scullory standing in a thicket just off to the porch. His face was all painted up like he was going to war and he had his rifle with him.

At that point I knew for certain I had been right about his intentions. I opened my mouth to call out, but Nathan silenced me with a glare and a finger held up over his lips. He shook his head slowly and in such a way that I knew he meant to do me harm if I said anything. I swallowed down my words and looked back towards my pa. He stood staring after the Squamate as it wound its way around our porch, its large clawed feet seeming at odds with the delicate steps it took as it scented the air, picking up a whiff of our warblers, I assumed. I looked back just in time to see Nathan disappear into the woods behind the thicket, headed off in the direction of the rear yard. His rifle glinted in the dim light as he entered the brush.

The Squamate was here to deal with the warblers

what infested our back shed, just as we had paid for it to do. It was doing its job, as different and even frightening as that job was. The Squamate terrified me, but in a way it was beautiful. It was special. I knew right then in my heart that I just couldn't let Nathan kill that animal.

The Squamate was still slowly weaving its way through our yard, almost swaying, gently back and forth in slow, flowing waves that extended from its nose through the tip of its long, snakelike tail when suddenly it lifted its head straight up, knocking the hat to the ground. It roared, a sound I still hear in my dreams, the bandanna falling from its mouth and revealing a huge, gaping maw full of sharp little white teeth below a nose that was nothing more than two small holes. It took off in a run for our shed, tearing its coat free to fall in pieces, fluttering to the ground like butterflies what just dropped dead.

Pa looked at me and said, "Dell, get in the house."

I nodded and went in the front door, but I went right through and came out the back. I had to get ahold of Nathan and stop him before he did harm to that poor, strange creature. If he killed it, its death would be on my shoulders, its blood on my hands. That debt that was just too much for me to bear on top of my old dog, Ginger.

I stepped cautiously out into the yard, alert for either Nathan or the Squamate, or both. I listened for a telltale gunshot that would mean the end of her poor life, for I knew somehow that our Squamate was a female. I near had a heart attack when there came a piercing cry from the back shed. All of a sudden something tore up through the roof, bits of shingles exploding outwards in its wake, before landing with a thud right directly in front of me.

It was a warbler, alright. First fresh one I'd ever seen. It had about a six, maybe six and a half foot wingspan made of huge, sickly pink, leathery wings run through with all sorts of dark red veins like bloody spider webs. A short, squat little body ended in a little nub of a tail between two huge thighs what led down to large, vicious claws. Above its ghastly looking breastbone, all raw angles and skin stretched taught over its bony ribs, its reedy little neck arched, ending in a massive head with a pointed black beak near two foot long and shaped like the scissors Ma sometimes used to cut our family's hair. Its small, beady red eyes were fixed open and there was blood all over it.

I stood there staring at it, unsure of what to do when there come another of those screams, followed by a roar and the sound of things being torn open and eaten. I stood stock-still with my heart beating in my ears like a marching band, unsure of what to do next. That was when my eye caught the glint of the setting sun off a rifle from the loft window of the barn. Nathan.

I made my way to the barn as quick as I was able and scrambled up the ladder and into the loft. The ruckus from outside was more than enough to cover what noise I had made. I saw Nathan, crouched low to the window, aiming his rifle in the direction of the back shed. I swallowed hard and gathered up my wits and all my courage before I approached him. I wouldn't let fear rule me the way I had when those things had gotten my dog. I would save the Squamate from a cruel and senseless death at the hands of a small minded boy what had some military schooling and done grown too big for his britches.

"Nathan!" I said in the most authoritative voice I could muster.

I saw the set of his shoulders change, so I knew he had heard me, but he kept his eyes out the window and his rifle at the ready. I approached him as calmly as I was able.

"Nathan Scullory, don't you harm that beast!" I said, trying to sound as threatening as Nathan himself had been earlier.

Nathan didn't move from his crouch, but he answered me that time.

"What's it to you, yellow belly?" Nathan growled.

I clenched my fists, angered by him in so many ways I was shaking.

"That there animal is on my property, paid good and proper to be here by my father. You will get up now and you will leave this place and you will not return or so help me god, Nathan Scullory, but you will be sorry."

I think I had finally got his attention, for he lowered the rifle and set it by the window frame. He stood up slowly, his back still to me. I noticed his fists were clenched, and by his posture I figured he was fixing to start a fight. I was willing to take pain for the things I believed in. I think I hoped that in some way, it might make up for my cowardice in leaving Ginger to be eaten by those things, a lonesome and painful death that my poor dog had not deserved.

I stood my ground, my back stiff and straight, fists balled up ready for a fight that never came.

Just as Nathan wheeled around to face me, there came a terrible crash and before I knew what was what, the Squamate stood before me. Her eyes were wild, face bloodied from her meal, bits of skin and sinew hanging from her dripping, knife-like teeth as well as her sharp claws. I turned and started to back away, heedless that I was backing straight towards Nate Scullory, who was between myself and the window. The Squamate looked at both of us, from one to the other, before letting out another terrifying roar and making straight for me, mouth open wide to show the void inside. My death lay in that void.

Time seemed to stop where it was and everything took on a strange sort of feel, like something out of a nightmare where you can't move and can't stop the doom what's coming for you even though you can see it, right there, plain as day.

It was then that Nathan Scullory did something that I will never in my life understand. He rushed forward and pushed me out of the path of the beast, not even pausing to pick up his gun for protection. He could have stood by and let that monster eat me up as a distraction while he went for his gun, shot it dead as he had always planned to do without me to stand in his way. He'd have been a hero and I'd have been killed. Two birds with one stone, as Ma would've said. But he didn't do that. Maybe it didn't even occur to him. It might've been the military training or it might've been something else, but Nathan Scullory saved my life that day.

When Nathan shoved me, I wheeled around backwards, trying to put distance between the Squamate and myself. I was turned around now so I could face the window, see the stars just beginning to peek out of the purple twilight above our farm. I tried to make my way over to the ladder what led down to the ground floor of the barn, supposing I could flee and get the attention of the Squamate's handlers, but I tripped over my own two feet and fell from the hay loft onto the dirt below, the wind knocked out of me.

I was gasping for breath, feeling like I might yet pass over, but even so I was unable to tear my eyes from the scene unfolding in the loft. Nathan stood before the Squamate, staring up at the creature, and she stared right back, her great big eyes fixed on what was in front of her. Nathan stood his ground and the beast wove from side to side slowly, fluidly like the predator she was, dancing an intricate dance of death. Her tail moved on its own accord, like it was a separate being entirely, dancing a quicker dance, the end flicking left and right like a dog catching a scent. The orangey light of the setting sun struck off the Squamate's scales and made her look for all the world like she'd been set ablaze. Dust motes and bits of hay, no doubt stirred up by my fall, danced in shafts of that fading orange sunlight filtering through the wide gaps in the floor of the loft.

It was through those gaps I watched as Nathan took a step towards the beast, seemingly fearless. Pushing me out of its path was possibly the bravest and most selfless act he had ever carried out. Maybe he had just wanted me out of the way so he could have at the beast, but I wanted to give him the benefit of the doubt. I couldn't see too well just then. My vision was swimming in and out of clarity, or maybe it was the fading light, but it looked to me like everything was underwater: fuzzy and a little shimmery, more distant than it should've been. And I felt cold. Very cold, for the warm May evening. I felt nigh on to freezing.

Nathan and the Squamate continued to dance their deadly dance without showing signs of stopping any time soon. I tried to cry out for someone, anyone, to come put a stop to it by any means necessary, but my voice stopped in a painful croak and wouldn't leave my throat.

TWENTY-ONE

Suddenly and without warning, the Squamate lunged forward and bit the head clean off Nathan's shoulders. I watched, not able to comprehend quite what had happened, as she stretched out her neck and swallowed in one gulp, reminding me of a snake. I could see the round shape of the head as it moved down her throat.

Nathan's body fell backwards in a still twitching heap as his blood filtered down through the cracks in the floorboards, dripping onto the hay just past my feet. It was then that I looked down and saw what had become of my own body.

When I had fallen, I must've caught the tines of the pitchfork I had leaned up against the bearing post that very day. It had plunged right through my thigh and broken. The handle lay on the ground beside me. My blood was everywhere, redder than the barn paint. It had broken my leg badly. I could see the jagged shards of bone, along with the three long iron spikes, poking out through my tattered and blood soaked overalls, but I couldn't feel it none. It should've hurt something terrible by the looks of it. I tried to move my toes and found I was unable. I couldn't move or feel my lower half at all. I tried again to scream, to call for help but I couldn't utter a sound. I raised my head to look for the Squamate when all the strength what was left in me bled out, turning the world to blackness, and I remembered no more.

EPILOGUE

That was many years ago, and much has happened since. Larry Scullory shot himself in the head with his son's own rifle on the night Nathan's funeral was held. Nathan's Ma went to live with some relations somewhere south of here soon after. Ma and Mabel returned from their stay with our own relatives sometime after the events of that tragic day. Pa could never look at me the same way again. I reckon at least somewhat on account of my part in what happened. As for myself, I won't never walk again without aid of a cane, and slowly at that. What use is a lame son to a farmer, born and bred?

I don't rightly know what happened to the Squamate. The warblers had been dealt with and I've never seen hide nor hair of one, nor heard their racket, since. Pa never would let on what had happened that night. I do know it was him what found me, but I know not in what condition. I woke up in my own bed with old Doc Redding looking over me more than a fortnight later. While I know I was the subject of many whisperings among the townsfolk, none were ever spoke where I could hear them.

Folk just didn't want to talk about it around me, I

guess. Just one of them things you have no choice but to come to accept.

I learned many an important lesson that summer, but the one what seems most pressing is this: Sometimes in life we are faced with no good option, only evil, and it's up to us to choose the lesser.

ABOUT THE AUTHOR

Amber Fallon lives in a small town outside Boston, Massachusetts that she shares with her husband and their two dogs. A techie by day and a horror writer by night, Mrs. Fallon has also spent time as a bank manager, motivational speaker, produce wrangler, and apprentice butcher. Her obsessions with sushi, glittery nail polish, and sharp objects have made her a recognized figure around the community.

Amber's publications include *The Terminal*, *Daughters of Inanna*, *So Long and Thanks for All the Brains*, *Daily Frights 2012*, *Women of the Living Dead*, *Zombie Tales*, *Here Be Clowns*, *Horror on the Installment Plan*, *Zombies For a Cure*, *Quick Bites of Flesh*, *Daily Frights 2013*, *Mirror, Mirror*, *Operation Ice Bat*, *Painted Mayhem*, and *Return to Deathlehem*.

For more information, please tweet her @Z0mbiegrl or visit her blog at www.amberfallon.net and listen to her podcast, *It Cooks*, on Project iRadio!

CPSIA information can be obtained
at www.ICGtesting.com
Printed in the USA
LVOW11s1434220817
545953LV00001B/2/P